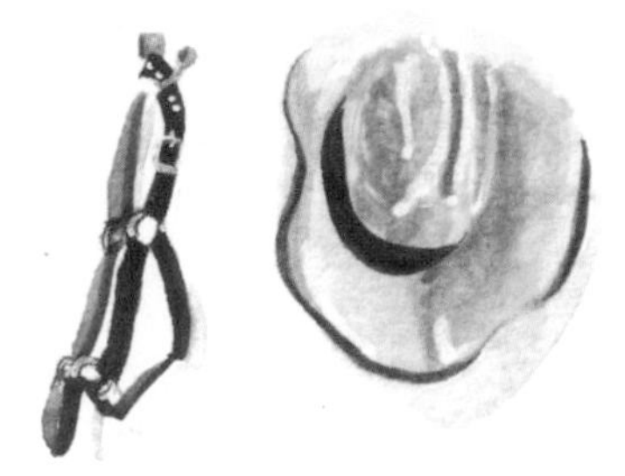

This book is written in memory of my brothers, Wade James Cooper (1967 – 2011) and Cameron Daniel Cooper (1971 – 2011) and dedicated to all the children who loved them, especially Bryn, Sam, Grace, Maggy, Ruben and Sandy. KC

For friendship – in all forms and colours, shapes and sizes. (And for Kate, without whom I may never have obsessively drawn horses as a child.) LE

Tundra Books, an imprint of Penguin Random House Canada Young Readers, a Penguin Random House Company

Library and Archives Canada Cataloguing in Publication

Cooper, Kelly, 1963-, author
If a horse had words / Kelly Cooper ; Lucy Eldridge, illustrator.

Issued in print and electronic formats.
ISBN 978-1-101-91872-2 (hardcover). —ISBN 978-1-101-91873-9 (EPUB)

I. Eldridge, Lucy, illustrator II. Title.

PS8605.O67I3 2018 jC813'.6 C2017-902620-8
C2017-902621-6

Published simultaneously in the United States of America by Tundra Books of Northern New York, an imprint of Penguin Random House Canada Young Readers, a Penguin Random House Company

Library of Congress Control Number: 2017939198

Edited by Elizabeth Kribs
Designed by Terri Nimmo
The artwork in this book was created with watercolor.
The text was set in Bembo.
Printed and bound in China

www.penguinrandomhouse.ca

1 2 3 4 5 22 21 20 19 18

Penguin Random House
TUNDRA BOOKS

IF A HORSE HAD WORDS

Kelly Cooper

Illustrated by Lucy Eldridge

tundra

The foal is born on a spring morning of sunshine and snowmelt. She opens her eyes and looks around. If she had words, she would say *willow*, *crocus*, *puddle* and *sky*.

She feels a quiver that ripples from her nose to her tail.

If a horse had words, the word would be . . .

up.

A newborn horse has to stand up.

Her legs are long and thin.
Legs for a spider, not a horse.

Her mother nudges her.

Stand up.

The little horse sets her two front hooves firmly on the grass and pushes with all her strength.

Up, she pushes. Up and forward.

She slips.

Her front legs scramble, trying to hold.

She is sliding. Backward. Even a newborn horse knows that backward is the wrong direction.

Stuck.

Her back legs are caught in a badger hole.

She struggles, but the soft and sandy earth holds tight around her flanks.

The little horse hears her mother's worried snorts.

She hears a hawk whistle high above.

In the distance, a low rumble vibrates through the earth, the awful earth that won't let her go.

Something is coming.
Something much bigger than a horse.

The foal's heart is pounding. Just as she thinks the great big Something is about to run right over her, it stops and spits two creatures out.

The large one is a man. And the small one?

If a horse had words,
the word would be . . .

boy.

The man drops a loop of rope over the foal's head.

She shakes her mane.

She wants it off.

"Shhhhhhh," the boy says.

The little horse holds her head still, listening.

A gentle sound, like the swish of a horse's tail. *Shhhhhhh*.

The man begins to pull. The boy puts his hands on the rope, adds his weight to the pulling. The foal feels the rope tighten. Then the ground that holds her starts to give.

All of a sudden, the earth lets go. And there they are, her two back legs.

She knows what to do.

With all her heart and all her strength, the little horse pushes herself out of the hole toward the sky.

The boy reaches out, quick as sunlight, and takes the rope from around her neck.

"Good work," the man says.

The little horse takes a few steps, wobbling and swaying, lifting her hooves as high as she can.

Her mother nickers softly. *Good work.*

The boy smiles. Then he turns toward the truck.

The foal watches him go, each step a jump, a leap as long and high as he can make it.

This boy. He doesn't like the ground either.

Hawk in the sky. A belly full of grass. The word for this is *summer*. *Fall* is leaf rustle and fence posts. Then *winter*. White hills and long nights. Horses standing close for warmth. The man and the boy bring food, hay full of dried flowers, a hint of sweet summer. Then *spring*. A belly full of grass again.

If a horse had words, the word would be . . .

SEASONS.

Seasons pass and the boy still loves the air.

Seasons pass and the horse still fears the ground.

She is tall now, has to bend her head to sniff the pocket of the boy's shirt. She smells something sweet and sharp and delicious.

"Hello, Red Badger."

If a horse had words, the word would be . . .

Name.

Her name is Red Badger. Because her hair is bright reddish-brown, the color of young chokecherry twigs in springtime. Because she slipped into a badger hole and the boy was there to save her.

He opens his hand. On his palm, a peppermint.

The boy blows a breath of greeting into her nostrils.
She nickers.

If a horse had words, the word would be . . .

friend.

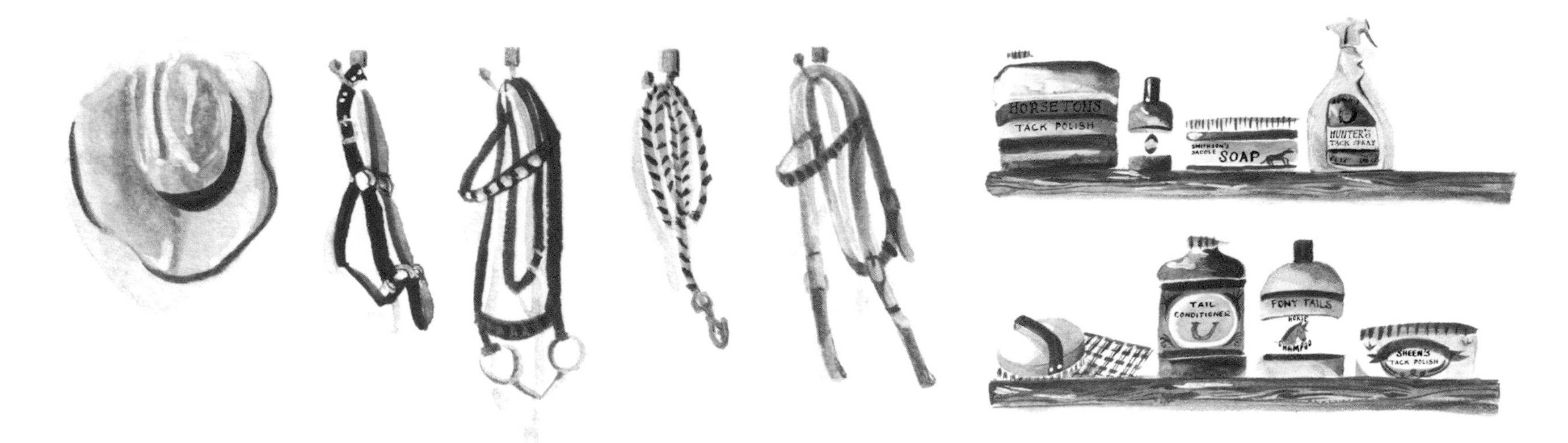

One day, the boy leads her to the corral.

He slips a bridle over her head.
He puts a saddle on her back.

Her feet sink into the soft dirt.
She fidgets beneath the saddle's weight,
shifting from side to side.

Red Badger doesn't like the ground,
but she loves the boy.

The boy climbs gently onto her back. He is skinny, light as a hawk's feather.

But if you are a horse who does not like the ground, any weight at all—even a hawk's feather—is too much.

Red Badger hops, trying to keep her feet in the air.
She kicks her back legs high, high above her head.

Suddenly, the weight is gone.

And the boy?

He is on the ground.

The boy stands up and brushes the dust from his hat.
He is laughing.

But the man was watching and he is not.

The horse does not understand what
the man is saying, but the boy does.

Red Badger has to go.

Red Badger does not understand this new place, these herds of people, their raised hands, the loud voice singing numbers. She prances into the small ring, head held high.

The ring man touches her back with his whip, softly, gently, just to guide her.

She bucks, then rears, her nose reaching for the sky.

If a horse had words, the word would be . . .

SOLD!

A new ranch. Red Badger and the other horses play hide-and-seek all winter among the willow trees. They kick at the clouds and snort wishes to the night stars. Snow falls and melts. Falls and melts again.

Time passes and the place where she was born slips further and further away.

But when she looks at the sky, she thinks of the boy.

If a horse had words, the word would be . . .

remember.

Welcome
TO THE
EYEHILL STAMPEDE

If you are a horse, the rodeo smells of
the oiled hinges of the bucking chutes and the
laundry soap of a cowboy's clean shirt.

The rodeo is movement. The fringe on
chaps and the tails of horses. Hooves thudding.
Hats tossed into the air.

Dirt and sky.

The cowboys who get on her back can't ride her.
Some who try are sharp. She throws them off.

Some are heavy. They go too.

Some are slim and light.

They don't make much noise when
they hit the ground.

When the horn blows, her saddle is empty.

The people in the crowd clap their hands together again and again. The sound is for the cowboys who try to ride her.

And for Red Badger, the bronc who bucks them off.

She is back in the chute, waiting.
She fidgets, lifts one hoof and then the other.

"Easy, girl. Shhhhhhh."

She snorts. *Boy? Is that you?*

She feels the rein tighten.
He eases his weight onto her back.
Soon the cowboys will open the gate.

She twists her head, trying to look up at him.
Again, his voice: “Red Badger? Is that you?”

The gate opens.

The horse leaps high. The boy hangs on.
They shoot into the air like fireworks.

Red Badger pricks up her ears. She can’t see the cowboy standing on the chute above her, but she knows that voice. Gentle, like the swish of a horse’s tail.

Her nostrils flare. She knows that smell.

Peppermints.

Red Badger whinnies.
The sound is a shout, sky-high and wild.

If a horse had words, the word would be . . .